The Fells Fairies

By Wendy Pfaffenbach

Artwork by Julian Peters

To Maya and Zoe —
May you always
keep exploring.

W. Pfaffenbach

Panther Cave Press
Dedicated to publishing authors with a strong
connection to Medford, MA
www.PantherCavePress.com

Book design by Jason Gray
Cover design by Jules Talbot

For my mother and father, who taught me to love the woods, and to my daughters and husband who walk in the woods with me.

Table of Contents

The Fells Fairies

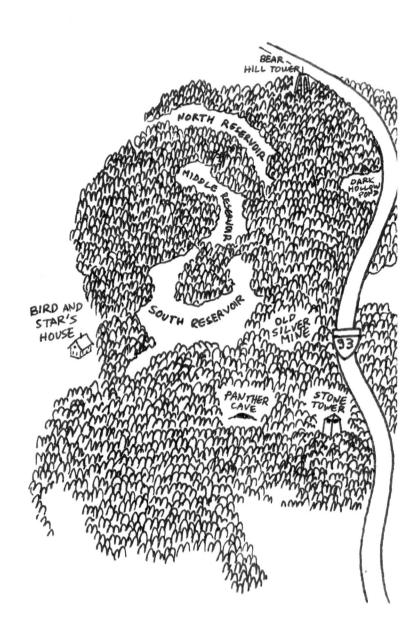

SPOT POND
RESERVOIR

GREAT
ISLAND

FELLS
RESERVOIR

WRIGHT'S
POND

THE FELLS

N

TO
BOSTON

CHAPTER ONE

The Fells

Star and Bird lived in a small white house with a steep roof that reached up for the sky and out toward the trees. The house was all angles and triangles with a few rectangles and a circular window at the top. If you looked in the window, you would see a purple, yellow, and blue room with two white beds, two white dressers, and two little girls jumping on the beds. When Star and Bird grew tired of jumping on the beds and looked out the window, they saw a giant park: The Fells. The Fells was 53 steps away from Bird and Star's front door (their parents had counted before buying the house). It was an old park with narrow paths that twisted over streams, dark mossy spots with ferns and pools, high dry spots with glimmering granite, and perfect places that smelled of pine and were covered in low-growing blueberries. Best of all, the Fells had rocks. Not ordinary rocks, but giant craggy boulders that appeared where you least expected them; mammoths that leaned against each other to form caves and mountains and ledges perfect for the adventures of little girls. Every Sunday, Star and Bird would walk in this park with their parents. In the fall, they collected acorn tops and leaves; in the winter, they skated on the frozen ponds; in the spring, they walked the paths looking for lady slippers, and in the summer, they hiked to the park's old stone tower and looked out over the woods and city. They did not know they were being watched.

The trees watched them pick up their leaves, the frozen pond observed them gliding silently across it, the lady slippers whispered to each other as the girls walked by, and when the girls climbed the tower, its old stones opened heavy eyes. Slowly, with each passing season, each part of the park began to think the same hopeful thought ... *Maybe*. The Fells was beautiful, and it was special. It had survived for hundreds of years. It watched as the nearby city swallowed the fields, cliffs, pools, and pines. Thirty years ago (not long at all if you are an oak tree) men had visited with maps and instruments and had cut a giant six-lane highway right through its center. Now, thousands of cars rushed by, sending exhaust into the air and killing any delicate flower that dared grow along the side. The Fells knew that the thousands of people who used its paths each year loved it, but the old forest also knew that they loved something else more. More than lightning or fire, the forest feared men with plans and bulldozers.

Maybe, the Fells thought as it watched the girls. *Maybe they will help.*

CHAPTER TWO

The Blueberries

"Put on your sneakers! Where is the bug spray?" Star and Bird's mom rushed around the house, shouting orders. "Where are the buckets? Star, have you been using them again to make concoctions? Wear socks. It's tick season." Like well-trained cadets, her daughters and husband arrived at the front door, bug spray in hand and socks on their feet. She looked them over and pushed them out the door. "Berries! Girls, we must go gather those blueberries."

"Hurry up, girls," their father smiled. "If the chipmunks eat them all, your mother will not be happy."

"Not fair," Star said, "The chipmunks didn't have to find their sneakers."

"If you'd put them in the hall," Bird started, but before she could finish Star shot her a look that made her swallow the rest of the sentence.

The family walked the 53 steps and entered the Fells. The forest hung over them, cool and damp; a few sun rays slipped through the leaves creating pale paths in the air. They walked along a stream and up a rocky hill past oaks and maples until they reached a pine grove. There, on top of a hill, the lowbush blueberries grew. The bushes covered a space the size of a large playground and one glance at their mother's face let them know that the bushes were covered with perfectly small, ripe, wild berries. They had beaten the chipmunks.

"We'll start in the middle and pick toward the edges," their mother said. "Your father and I will go to the right. You head off to the left."

The girls rushed to the far side of the berry patch and began picking. Bird glanced up occasionally to check on her parents who were crouched low concentrating on the berries. Each time she glanced up, her parents were farther and farther away from her. She moved through her own patch searching, picking, and dropping berries into her bucket. She glanced up again, and just as her parents disappeared behind a slope of small pines, Bird felt a breeze move through the woods. She looked up to find her parents. They were gone. Every part of the forest seemed more bright, more clear, and more still. She squinted, not as one usually does to clear her sight, but instead to adjust to this new clarity.

Bird shook her head, "Come on," she said, gesturing to the far left of the berry patch. "Let's move over there."

Star, who always said whatever was on her mind, opened her mouth to talk about the feeling, but found no words. "Okay," she said, and started to hum along with the sounds in the forest. Bird joined her and the two made up a song about summer, blueberries, and whatever had happened yesterday. They sang, and picked, and looked up at the forest, neither quite sure what to say about the magic surrounding them. Their buckets were a quarter full of berries when Star jumped into the air.

She landed in a crouch and waved her sister next to her. Bird looked down suspiciously and then played along.

Star's eyes were wide and her arm shook slightly as she pointed. "Did you see that?"

"What?" asked Bird.

"I saw a flying doll." Star shook her head and grabbed her sister's arm.

Bird arched her eyebrows and pursed her lips. She was used to her little sister's dramatic outbursts. "Star, you saw a big dragonfly. Stop it." Star shook her head and her grip tightened.

"Well," Bird ventured, "was it a butterfly?"

"I know it's not a butterfly," Star pouted, she'd written an extensive report about butterflies in school that year. "Its body is too long, and its wings are too pointy." The wind picked up again.

"Shhh," Bird whispered. "Do you hear something?"

The two girls froze. The breeze danced around them.

"*Hello, hello, hello,*" the wind chimed.

"Was that a bell?" Star asked.

"Maybe someone's windchimes?" Bird whispered. "Shhhh. Listen."

"Greetings." It chimed again, this time shaking the blueberry bushes.

"It's coming from the ground," Star said as she bent even lower over the berries and peered through the tangle of thin branches. "Nothing," she said, but when she stood slightly, something fluttered close to her nose. And, when she stood up completely, she dropped her entire bucket of berries. There, in the center of the berry patch stood Bird, still as a statue, the wind gently lifting her long brown hair, her eyes fixed in amazement at the creature hovering six inches in front of her face.

"Hello," the creature said again. Its voice echoed out like a silver chime. "Can you hear me?"

Bird nodded her head slowly. Star crept across the berry patch to stand by her sister. Once at her side, she clasped Bird's hand. It was only then that Bird looked over at Star.

"Well, can you hear me?" the creature asked again, addressing Star with an impatient smirk on his face.

"Yes," Star's voice sounded scratchy. "What are you?"

"Silly question," the creature replied. "You know exactly what I am."

"You're a fairy," said Bird.

"We prefer 'spirit,' more modern, but if you like fairy, it's close enough," the fairy replied. The girls shuffled their feet, unsure of what to say next.

The fairy cleared his throat, "I've been sent by the forest." The fairy seemed to think this would explain everything, but the girls just looked on blankly. The fairy tried again, "I've been sent by the forest because it needs your help."

"I'm sorry," interrupted Bird.

"Who is the forest?" Star asked. "What is your name?"

"I was afraid of this," the fairy shook his head. "Extremely disappointing. You two are as thick as thawed mud in March. We're going to have to do this the old-fashioned way." He took a small green bag from the pocket of his shirt.

Bird and Star had watched their fair share of fairy movies, so they knew exactly what was in that little green bag. They looked at each other and started shaking with excitement. "Are you thinking what I'm thinking?" Star whispered to Bird.

"Fairy dust!" they both exclaimed.

"Does it really exist?" Bird asked, her eyes shining.

"Does it really exist," the fairy grumbled. "I'm sent on a mission to save the natural world and the humans are more excited about visiting Neverland." The fairy reached into the purse and pulled out a handful of dirt.

"Dirt? Why are you carrying a handful of dirt?" Star didn't try to hide her disappointment.

"This isn't dirt," the fairy said. "It is fairy dirt. If I hit you with a few granules of this and you can fly for hours."

"We thought it was called fairy dust," Bird said politely, trying to hide her extreme disappointment that the magical world had so far supplied them with a grumpy fairy and a bag of dirt.

"Yeah, well, it isn't. It's fairy dirt. But do you humans accept that dirt is magical? No. It has to be golden, it has to sparkle," the fairy was getting very worked up. "Can you grow food from gold? What does gold give you? Nothing! Then how on earth, and I mean Earth, could it generate magic!" The fairy sat and harrumphed.

"We're sorry," Bird said in her calmest voice. "That looks like very nice fairy dirt."

"It's the best," the fairy replied, coming to his senses. "Watch." And he threw the dirt right into Star's eyes.

"Hey! You could make her go blind," Bird said, reaching for her sister. "You never throw dirt in someone's eyes." The fairy looked at her and laughed.

"Of course, we throw dirt in someone's eyes. How else can we get her to see?" he asked and then pointed to Star who was looking around with an expression Bird had only seen before on Christmas morning.

"It's all alive," Star said to herself. She reached up to the sky and then bent low to the bushes.

"Next the ears," the fairy said, matter-of-factly tossing dirt into Star's ears. "No one ever accomplished anything good without some dirt in his ears." Star sat upright, and leaned her ear to the breeze, then she started humming along with a song Bird couldn't hear. "You too," he said, turning and tossing dirt into Bird's eyes and ears.

The two girls stood among the berry bushes and saw the forest for the first time. They saw what they had always known was there but had never experienced. They saw each part: the ladybugs on the blueberry leaves, the blue jay in the oak, the leap of the squirrel, the thick grey oak bark, and they also saw it all fit together as a whole.

Star said, "It's like when we've been working on a puzzle for a whole afternoon and then after one tough piece, the last 20 or so just fall into place."

"Yes," Bird said. "But it's real … I think."

They looked at the fairy who smiled as if something else was coming, and, of course, it was.

Star screamed. Bird looked over and saw that her sister's feet were hovering above the ground.

"She's floating!" she exclaimed.

"It should be flying. Pretty poor performance," the fairy observed, then he pointed at Bird's feet.

She was flying too. The two girls rose up into the air until they were as high as the top of the oaks, but they wriggled and kicked, unable to maneuver their bodies through the air. Bird tried pointing her arms straight like she'd seen in a superhero movie, but she just turned awkwardly as if she were rolling down a bumpy hill. Star tried backflips and, much to her astonishment, found that her gymnastics improved greatly when she wasn't hampered by gravity. "Check me out," she yelled to her sister. "Do you think I'm a level six?" Bird rolled her eyes at her sister and ignored her aerial tricks. Instead, she concentrated, as she always did, on the task at hand.

"Star," she reminded her sister, "shouldn't you be concentrating on learning how to fly instead of gymnastics?" Star shrugged and flipped a bit farther away from her boring sister.

"I've got it," Bird said. "Just treat the air like it is water … swim!" Bird tried to kick off from the top of the tree like she would the bottom of a pool. It worked! Next, she dove toward the top of the tree and pushed off into the air. Star looked over and immediately started an elegant breaststroke, skimming over the forest.

Star flipped and spun and cartwheeled while Bird swam through the air. Eventually, the two collided and started an impromptu game of salt and pepper, holding each other's hands and pushing and pulling each other up and down over the tops of the trees.

The fairy hovered above the patch with his arms crossed and the corners of his mouth turned down. He glared up at the laughing girls who had just declared this the best day of the whole summer. His frown deepened and his eyes darkened. Completely exasperated would have described only the better part of his mood. "Enough!" he called.

The girls returned to the fairy and hovered in front of him. Suddenly, Star looked at the fairy and laughed in an embarrassed way. "I'm sorry," she said, "What is your name?"

"You can call me Jasper," the fairy replied. "But enough of this, we have work to do."

CHAPTER THREE

The Smogrots

From the top of the oak tree the girls could see the surrounding landscape. They saw the neighborhood that held their crooked house, the parks they played in, and their school. They also saw the city, with its bridge that opened like a book, and the harbor. They saw the Fells, all green and grey, a garden for everyone. They saw the giant highway slicing through the garden and the cars rushing back and forth, to and from the city. They also saw something they had never seen before: oddly shaped clouds in various shades of murk covering the landscape.

"Do you see those things?" Bird asked Star.

Star shook her head, "They look like oily clouds."

"They look like Play-Doh after it's been used too much, and the colors are all mashed together," Bird observed. "I've never seen them before."

"Of course, you've never seen them before." Jasper interrupted. "You can't see them unless you've got the dirt in your eyes. And, if you think they look bad," he added. "Wait until you smell them."

"What are they?" Star asked.

"We call them smogrots, don't know what they call themselves. We first saw them about 100 human-years ago. They are why you are here."

"Excuse me?" Bird asked.

"Them," Jasper pointed. "You are here because of them."

"I'm not trying to be rude," Star said, which is always what she said before she said something she thought might be rude, "but what are you talking about?"

"Useless," Jasper muttered to himself. "I told Brian this was all useless, but does he listen to me?" Then he looked up, obviously disappointed, and quicker than the girls ever thought anything could move, he grabbed their wrists and flung them through the forest.

The girls hurtled right toward a large smogrot. As they flew closer, they saw that it wasn't a cloud at all. Instead, it was made up of what looked like thousands of dirty dish rags, but each dish rag had legs, and arms (if that is what you could call them), and a small mouth that seemed to screech, howl, and hiss in a very strange, very low voice.

"We're flying into a cloud of mutated rats!" Bird screamed.

"Lizard Barbie dolls! What's that smell?" Star gagged.

The girls hurtled closer to the swarm of greasy, stinky, angry creatures.

"We need to stop him," Bird screamed.

"How? We can't land on our feet and we're heading straight for the highway!" Star screamed back. The girls screamed louder as the pavement and the cloud of smogrots came closer and closer.

"Brace yourself!" Jasper shouted, as he skidded to a stop five feet from the side of the road and casually shoved the sisters right into the smogrots.

At first, they were fascinated by the creatures. The smogrots were not all alike, some looked like dirty rags, while others were like wisps of filthy tissue, brown, grey, mustard yellow with tinges of green. Each had a tiny misshapen face that reminded Bird of a Halloween project she'd done in art one year when she'd carved a face into an apple and then left it out to dry for a week. They moved in schools, like fish, around the dark grey center that whirled like a mini-tornado. Star reached her hand into the center. When she took it out, it was covered with grime and smelled like a gas station on a humid day.

"This isn't so bad," Star said, looking at her dirty fingernails.

"You're right," Bird replied. "It kind of stinks, and they're certainly ugly, and the sound they make would be terrible if it were louder, but all-in-all, I don't see what the big deal is." The girls moved along with the smogrots. Occasionally, one would brush up against their clothes leaving a smudge of grime, or one would come close to an ear and hiss or howl. Still, the girls thought that the smogrots were more annoying than dangerous.

Bird turned to Jasper, "These are kind of stinky and ugly, but what's the big deal?"

He stared at her in disbelief. "These are kind of stinky and ugly, but what's the big deal," he mocked. "Typical human," and he spat at his feet in disgust. Bird shrugged.

The girls walked through the smogrots, undetected by the people driving by (they could see neither the smogrots, or the girls because they had no dirt in their eyes), until Bird stopped. "Did you see that?" she asked Star.

"See what?" Star said, looking ahead.

"Look at the Queen Anne's Lace," Bird ordered, pointing to the white flowers growing along the side of the road. "Watch." As the girls moved past the flowers, they watched them change; they became less glossy, less alive. They lost the glimmer that the dirt-sight had allowed the girls to see and just looked duller, sadder, more regular.

Bird looked at her sister and her eyes widened. Star was covered in a grime, but it was as if the grime had robbed Star of her shimmer too. She looked like she had the flu. Her hair was flat, her eyes were hollow, and her skin was a terrible shade of yellow.

"I don't feel good," Star said, pointing to the flowers. "Get me out of here." It was then that Bird realized she didn't feel well either.

"Jasper!" she called. "Get us out of here!" Before she even finished the silent "e" in here, the fairy reached his hands into the center of the smogrots, and the girls went flying out, landing in a ditch on the side of the road.

CHAPTER FOUR

The Curse of the Smogrots

"For the love of disco pants, what were those things?" Star asked.

"Funny you should ask," Jasper glared at the girls. "Why should you care?" He lifted his voice to a squeaky imitation of Bird, *"They're smelly but not dangerous,"* and he spat at his shoes again.

"Seriously, Jasper, tell us," Bird pleaded, still feeling a little sick.

"We're not entirely sure," he replied. "Weren't you listening? We call them smogrots, not quite sure what they call themselves." Jasper paused to spit at the cars as they rushed by.

"You already told us that," Star demanded. "We need to know more."

"You must know more than that," Bird arched her eyebrows. She believed in explanations.

Jasper shrugged. "We know that the smogrots first appeared when the people built houses. They weren't much of a problem at first, just hovered around the garbage heaps, sometimes even disappeared for months, years. Over the last 50 human years though, they've multiplied. Once this highway was built, they started hurting life on the edges. Now, some days they're in the whole forest." Jasper stopped talking, this time when he looked out at the cars his face curled into a tight grimace. He threw a pebble at the windshield of a truck.

"Jasper!" the girls screamed together. "You can't do that!"

"Why not?" the fairy screamed back, "Look what they've done to us." He swept his arm along the side of the road. The scene was dismal. Stalks of dried mustard-colored grass poked up through shredded plastic bags, soda bottles, and empty potato chip packages. Jasper's face was wrinkled and red with fury. "What's the difference? Every day your lousy species destroys a small part of my world." He glared at the girls.

"He's right," Bird observed. "We are destroying the planet. I just didn't realize we were destroying it so close to home." Jasper reached for another pebble. "Wait! Just because you're right doesn't mean you can break some-one's windshield," Bird took the rock from the fairy.

Star looked at Jasper and reached out her hand. She knew exactly how it felt to want to throw rocks at people.

"Jasper," she said, "I'm a bit of an expert at always getting in a little instead of a lot of trouble. Want to hear a silly song I made up to bother my parents when they drive? It's really funny." The fairy's face cleared, and he looked at the little blonde girl who added, "I bet you could really annoy some people by singing it."

CHAPTER FIVE

The Fairy Queen

After Jasper had mastered the tune and created a little dance to go with it, Star turned to her sister, "Come on, " she said. "We've got to get back to Mom and Dad. I bet they are losing their minds looking for us."

"You can't go back yet," Jasper interrupted. "I haven't introduced you to the spirit who sent me here."

"Who is that?" the girls asked.

"The fairy queen," Jasper answered, turning and flying up into the air. The girls flew after Jasper as fast as their amateur flying skills could take them.

"What did you say?" they shouted.

"The fairy queen. Hurry up."

"Wait. There really is a queen of the fairies?" Bird asked. Bird had spent hours of her life playing with her fairy dolls, making castles, villages, and houses, but she never allowed herself to believe that a fairy queen actually existed.

"You, of all children, should know that," Jasper replied. "You've been making houses for her for years."

"It's true," Star observed. "You turned the whole back porch into a fairy land."

"She especially liked the watering can cottage you made last summer," Jasper added. "It was very considerate of you to draw that beautiful Persian carpet for her bedroom."

Bird hovered in the sky, her mouth open and eyes wide. "This explains why everything was always moving," she whispered to herself.

"You can say sorry now," Star sassed. (Bird had accused Star of rearranging the village.) Bird opened her mouth to speak. "Apology accepted," Star smiled, "now, hurry up!"

CHAPTER SIX

What Goes On in a Little Girl's Mind?

There are stupid questions, and asking, *What goes on in a little girl's mind?* is one of them, because, as any little girl can tell you, each little girl has a mind of her own. If you could have peered into Bird's mind, you would have seen plans. Her mind shaped the world into her own designs: straight lines and curved windows and floors and maps for places that didn't exist. She dreamt of hallways that led into rooms with lofty ceilings, and winding paths that led to tiny huts where she could sit and play. When Bird looked at a rock she didn't think *rock*, she thought, *How can I use this to build something?* The same went for cardboard, scraps of ribbon, bark, leaves, sticks, unused cucumber trellises, and anything else that her mother left out in the rain. Bird built whole worlds, small cabins and even castles. She'd been building these worlds before she could even write or draw a proper person. And, she built every single one for the fairies.

Star too used anything that came her way. Everything had a purpose other than the boring one adults claimed it had. Coffee filters were fans, Q-tips were barrettes, each block in the Jenga game was actually a tiny person, if you just drew a face. Star's mind wove and darted and spun around any obstacle or object that came her way. She flitted from one creation to the next. One day she was a master sorceress mixing together perfumes in her mother's herb garden, the next she wrote a book that she stitched together herself, and the next she spent the whole day flipping cartwheels across the backyard. And, because she was the younger sister of someone who loved to build orderly worlds, she loved to add a bit of chaos to any scene she entered. Although the girls didn't know it, the fairies found them and needed them because of their very different minds.

The girls had hiked all over the Fells, and thought they knew its every nook and path, but Jasper led them down trails they had never seen before. He'd dart behind a fallen tree or a boulder and suddenly a new path would appear. Both girls were starting to get dizzy when the fairy finally stopped.

"Here we are!" he smiled. It was the first time either girl had heard happiness in his voice.

"We've been here a million times!" Star exclaimed. "We're at Panther Cave." Bird shook her head in agreement.

"There's no fairy castle here, " she stated. "I've explored every part of these rocks."

"Silly girls," Jasper chortled. "You think that you can find a fairy house at a location. You reach a fairy house by going down the right paths in the right way, not by finding the right address. Look."

There it was, just like the fairy castles Bird had been building for years. It had levels and angles. Pots of house-plants in bright red and blue ceramic pots sat on wire and wooden shelves, silver baskets and wicker baskets hung off of painted branches, and crystals and bells were draped like streamers across the whole arrangement, uniting it all. Inside there were tiny fires burning in tea-cups, soft beds made of cotton balls placed in old velvet jewelry boxes, and floors lined with pieces of yellow and gold stationery. The parts harmonized into a magically humming whole.

"Do you feel that?" Bird asked.

"I feel like my whole body is humming," Star observed. "I thought the sound was ...", but Star was interrupted by Bird's scream.

"You're shrinking!" Bird exclaimed.

"You are too!" The girls had no time to contemplate their new size, as a voice rang out from the enormous castle (which looked even more magnificent now that the girls could go inside).

"Girls, please, we invite you to enter our castle," the voice called, sounding like the chimes the girls' mother hung by their front door.

"Go!" Jasper ordered, shoving them between the entrance plants, and leading them down a seashell path. "The main hall is …"

"I know where the hall is," Bird whispered excitedly. "This is just like the castle I built last summer." She grabbed Star's hand and led her between two yellow flower pots. There, at the end of a green painted corridor, the queen sat on a throne made of silver spoons and tinsel. She wore a long blue gown, cinched at the waist and covered with tiny stars. Over her shoulders, she draped a golden shawl. Every part of her sparkled and glowed. Her dark brown hair was pulled up into a loose bun, and she looked down at the girls with black shining eyes and a kind smile.

"It's about time we got a *real* fairy," Star whispered to Bird.

"Star and Bird," she said, "Thank you for visiting my hall. And, Bird, thank you for all the beautiful houses you have made for me and my people. The one on your back porch last summer was particularly magnificent. I loved how you used your mother's best cucumber trellis to suspend the unicorn stables above the main dwelling. It is because of that great thoughtfulness and insight that I have called you here." Bird stood straighter, feeling proud of the hours she spent creating her castle. "And," the fairy continued, "Star, you might not have realized it, but my people and I bathed in all those potions you made from your mother's garden. The lavender, coneflower, and bee balm was my personal favorite. We also watched you dancing in the backyard. For some time last summer, my courtiers copied your moves. It is because of your energy and creativity that I have called you here." Star too felt a surge of confidence when the queen spoke.

"Thank you," they stammered.

"You may not be thanking me when your adventure is over," the queen said, looking seriously at them. "But enough, come and join me for tea." She snapped her wings back and forth and a mismatched tea set of acorn tops, Sacagawea dollars, and broken lockets appeared in front of the girls.

Bird instantly recognized the tea set as one of her own creations. "I made that," Bird whispered to Star, as they approached the table. The table was covered with their favorite treats, their grandmother's cinnamon buns, their mother's raspberry jam sugar cookies, and an open jar of Nutella with two spoons stuck inside. When the

queen poured the tea from the hollowed-out acorn, Star gasped in delight.

"That's my mint and bee balm recipe!" she exclaimed, taking a sip. "You even added the right amount of honey." She did a little wiggle dance in her chair, a sign that she was happier than happy.

The queen laughed, "Don't be so amazed girls, we have been watching you for a while. We've been looking for a certain kind of child to help us. We've needed to find a replacement for our trusted Brian for some time. But the right child is so hard to find these days." Star rolled her eyes, thinking that the fairy was going to start talking about how terrible children were these days.

"What do you mean?" Bird asked. "Aren't most children good?"

The queen frowned. "Of course, most children are good," she replied. "But I didn't say good. I said 'right.' A good child wouldn't have helped us at all. A good child would have asked us what the rules were and worried about breaking them. A good child would try to please me. Good children are fine for crowded classrooms, playgrounds, and large family gatherings, but we needed *you*."

"Hey! Are you saying we're bad kids?" Star blurted out through a mouthful of Nutella. "You sound just like my mom when she's really telling me I've done something bad, but at first it sounds like she's just talking about choices or other kids."

Bird shook her head in agreement, "Tricky grown-up talk."

"You are not bad," the fairy explained. "Some grown-ups might think so, but that is only because they lack spirit. What I'm saying is," she paused to think here, "you are more like a fairy. You'll follow a rule if it is just in the circumstances. You rush toward your play with an enthusiasm that can't be corralled by schedules or dinners, and you fight mightily when you feel you've been wronged."

Bird turned to Star with a silly grin on her face, "I'm not quite sure, but I think the fairy queen just said we are sassy." Star giggled because, truth be told, she knew her sister was right.

The fairy queen sat up and looked with an intent ferocity into the girls' eyes, "Whatever you are, you will need every drop of it to stop the smogrots."

"What?" the girls asked.

"I have summoned you here to stop the smogrots. Although humans cannot see them, I have come to believe that humans created them, and somehow the smogrots and certain humans are working together to destroy the Fells. Our trusted Brian has protected us for many years now, but we need new children. Star and Bird, the Fells

Fairies are depending on you. You must contact Brian and take over his work. The last time Brian visited he could hardly find the path to my castle. Once he was here he reported that the Fells, the last refuge we have in this land, is under attack again." The queen's voice rose as she spoke and her eyes filled with tears. "It appears that the humans have taken the form of something called The Green Corporation, and they are planning to build a shopping mall and a road in the center of our home."

"I'm not trying to be rude," Bird suggested in her nicest voice, "but I'm pretty sure that's impossible. My mom says that the Fells is protected."

"Don't grown-ups have laws to take care of important places?" Star asked.

"We thought we were protected too," the queen said sadly, "and yet it appears that this new form of Green Corporation has powers that are greater than the protections we thought we had. We need your help."

"Ms. Fairy Queen," Bird interrupted. "We'd love to help, but we're just kids. We've got camp and piano and art projects and basketball."

"Plus," Star added, "We have no idea where to begin. You need to find some big and powerful grown-ups."

"And, we don't have any money or power," Bird added. "We can't even vote. Last year, when I tried to start a petition to extend recess, the principal just ignored me."

Jasper appeared at the door to the throne room and walked to the table. He turned to the queen, "Told you it was useless," he grumbled, and pointed to the girls as if they couldn't understand what he was saying. "We might as well hand them a screen and start looking for a new place to live."

"Girls," the queen asked, "do you love the Fells?" The girls paused. They'd never thought about loving a piece of land before.

"Well," Star answered, "I like climbing over the rocks and picking blueberries and walking around the pond in the spring."

"And, I couldn't imagine how boring all those Sunday afternoons would have been if Mom and Dad hadn't brought us here."

"What would your childhood have been like without the Fells?"

Neither girl had ever thought about her childhood, as they were both in it—but for both this question created a sad feeling.

"It's weird," Star replied, "but when you ask me that I just feel like someone cut a hole in the center of one of my drawings." Bird shook her head in agreement.

"You are the only hope. Without you, the Fells will fall." The whole morning had been crazy, and both girls felt like they were in some kind of extended blueberry induced daydream; still, when they looked at the queen, they both felt the same word rise within them: Try. The word acted like a switch, and they knew then that they didn't even need to agree. They just needed to get to work.

"Okay," Star said, "who is this Brian?" At that moment, the queen faded away and the girls found themselves outside of Panther Cave.

"He's a friend of your father's," Jasper said, enjoying the look of shock on the girls' faces as they found their bearings in this new place.

"And, what are we supposed to do to stop this whole thing?" Star asked.

"What kind of plan do you want us to follow?" Bird added.

Jasper flew straight at her nose and looked at her as if she had just said something crazy like kids don't need summer vacation.

"Ugh!" he shouted, and a bit of his fairy spit hit her nose. "Are you turning obedient? Are you turning good? What is wrong with you? If the fairies knew how to stop this thing we wouldn't go looking to you! Didn't you hear anything the queen said? Use what you have, and figure it out for yourself!" And, leaving the scent of exasperation behind him, he disappeared.

CHAPTER SEVEN

Brian

The girls returned to the blueberry patch with seconds to spare. Their father had just pulled out his cell phone, and their mother was standing in the center of the bushes looking completely distraught. The parents rushed their children and asked many questions that needed to be artfully dodged, before finally scolding and lecturing about staying together and keeping an eye on the time. The girls felt terrible, but they also felt the great need to return home to discuss the events of the day.

As soon as they reached home, the girls rushed up the stairs and locked the door to their bedroom.

"What is this?" their mother called. "Aren't you going to beg for television or to go to a friend's house?" The girls did not answer and their mother shrugged it off as another stage of development she had never heard of.

They reappeared at dinner, when the conversation went like this:

"Dad, do you have a friend named Brian?" Star asked. Their father, shocked that his youngest daughter had taken an interest in his life, exchanged a confused glance with his wife before answering.

"Yes, you've even met him, Mr. Ridge, the retired biologist who substitute-teaches at the high school." The girls became noticeably excited, prompting another confused glance between the parents.

"Is he nice?" Bird asked. Unable to believe that a retired biologist was still the subject of conversation, their father paused a bit too long before answering.

"Very. You've met him a number of times, and when you were little you even went to his 60th birthday party. I can show you pictures after dinner."

"Can we meet him again?" Star asked, her eyes gleaming with excitement. At this point, the parents stopped eating entirely.

"Let me get this straight," their mom said, placing her fork next to her plate in a way that commanded total attention. "You want us to schedule you a playdate with a 60 year-old retired biologist?"

"Yes! We'd like that," the girls chimed, which caused their mother to ask if they were feeling well.

"Why?"

The girls exchanged a quick glance. They were often naughty, but somehow neither wanted to tell a real lie to their parents, and they both knew that they could never tell a grown-up about the fairies. Bird nodded to her little sister, in the way only one sister can communicate with another, the nod signaled that this explanation was Star's department. She smiled her biggest gap-toothed smile and looked her mother straight in the eyes. "Well, Mom," she explained, "while we were in the Fells today we realized that there was a lot to it." She paused here, considering if she should add something about learning. "We just thought it would be cool to know something more about it."

Her mother's suspicion continued. "You, child of sequins and cartwheels, you want to know more about a land preserve?" Star shook her blonde curls and gazed sweetly at her parents. It was Bird's turn.

"We really do!" she urged. "Today I was just thinking that if I knew more about the flowers and the rocks I could make my houses look more natural." Her parents believed this. "And, she added, going too far, "maybe he knows something neat like what kinds of dinosaurs lived there."

"I don't know about the dinosaurs," her father said, "but I, for one, am very pleased that you girls are taking an interest in your community. I was going to see Brian about a few photographs he took of the wildflowers in the Fells that your mother liked. I'll call him after dinner and see if we can set up an earlier meeting."

The next day, their father drove them to Brian's house for an afternoon tea. The house was a pale yellow with blue and white trim, and, much like their own, it wore its spirit on the outside. It was an old cape with add-ons that created unexpected nooks and angles. Instead of grass, wildflowers grew in the front yard strewn among rocks and small shrubs. "It looks like Brian has constructed his own Fells," Bird observed. There were bluebird houses in the trees and a fountain with a little girl standing watering flowers. "She's a fairy," Bird whispered, and when Star looked more closely, she noticed the small wings on the girl's back.

"I bet she's a lot nicer than Jasper," Star whispered back.

"Come on girls," their father called. "If I know Brian, he's out in his garden." Their father followed a field stone path around the side of the house into a garden much like the one in the front, only larger, with winding paths that led to arbors with benches, and the sound of water from fountains the girls couldn't see yet. A spritely older man sat under a pergola in the center. In front of him was a table set with china and a silver teapot. He was reading a book with flowers on the front.

"What a pretty flower," Star exclaimed, running toward Brian. Star rarely waited for formal introductions.

"Looks like a flower, doesn't it?" Brian replied, "But it's actually glass."

"We saw those!" the girls remembered, "At the museum this winter." And they were off, talking of flowers and museums, music and gardens, spilling tea and eating vanilla cookies covered with lemon frosting and tiny tarts full of blueberries and whipped cream. Eventually, when the table was covered with crumbs and the teacups were empty, Brian and their father began talking about Brian's photographs, so the girls excused themselves to wander the garden.

Once they'd found a bench near the back of the garden, Star glanced over to Bird with a worried look, "How are we going to mention the fairies?"

"I'm not sure," Bird said.

"Aren't you worried? We have gobs of work to do." Star, who never worried about anything, was getting anxious.

"No," Bird said, surprising herself. "I just feel like this garden will help us." They looked up and saw their father and Brian walking towards them.

"Girls, does this garden remind you of anything?" their father asked.

"Of course, Dad," Bird replied, a little annoyed that her father would ask such an obvious question. "It looks like a tiny version of the Fells."

"Only fancier," Star said. "Like someone gave it a makeover."

"And without anyone trying to build ugly condos and shopping malls in it," Brian observed sadly.

The girls saw their chance. Bird didn't like lying, but she decided it would be weird if an 8-year-old girl knew the details of a local building project, so she asked, "Why would anyone want to build a shopping mall in the Fells? How would anyone get to it?"

Brian's blue eyes lost a bit of light when he replied, "They'll build an access road, right through the center of the Fells."

The girls gasped. The fairy queen had told them there was a problem, but they didn't realize it would be so bad.

"Who would do such a thing?" Star asked.

"They call themselves developers," Brian replied. "They claim that the new buildings and roads will bring a new shopping experience to the people of Boston."

"We don't need more shopping!" Bird cried, "We need to play in the Fells."

At this, her father laughed, "Is this my daughter arguing that kids need to play outside instead of on a screen?"

he asked in amazement. His daughters ignored him, focusing on Brian.

Without thinking, Star blurted out, "What can we do to help?" Brian looked at the two girls and stood silently.

"Do you mean it?" he asked. "Would you really like to help?"

"This is a big responsibility, girls," their father interjected. "Don't make a promise you can't keep."

The girls looked knowingly at each other; if only their father knew how many promises they'd already made!

"We mean it," they said.

CHAPTER EIGHT

A Fight on Two Fronts

"To stop the construction of the road and the mall we have to gather 5,000 signatures by the end of the month," Brian said. "If we can bring enough signatures to the court, we can get the judge to temporarily order a stop to the construction. This will give us time to create a case against the developers."

"But," Bird asked again, "I still don't understand. Why would anyone want to build shops in the Fells? Our town is already full of malls. We have big malls, strip malls, and big box stores with giant parking lots."

"But we only have one Fells!" Star interrupted. Bad things made Bird sad, but they just made Star angry. "Oh, this makes me so furious. I just can't control myself," she said as she stomped off to a far corner of the garden; she was old enough now to know that sometimes, especially when she was angry, she was better off expressing her anger to the trees and stones.

Star's dad looked around awkwardly, not sure what to say. "It seems like your daughters have strong feelings for the nature preserve," Brian offered.

"Yes," their dad answered, and he told Brian why they had bought their house, so close to the city and also surrounded by the woods. Star was throwing pebbles into a lily pond. He nudged Bird, "Why don't you go help your sister calm down?"

Bird was going to tell him that was a crazy idea, but one look at his face and she knew that she had better do what her father said. When she reached the lily pond, Star was bending low over a tiny statue, hidden in a stand of bee balm and coneflowers.

"I love the smell of bee balm," Bird observed, and rubbed a fuzzy leaf between her fingers, "It's spicy and sweet." Her sister didn't respond. "You know it's rude to ignore someone," she leaned down to shake her sister, and then she saw what her sister saw.

"Can you believe it? What does this mean?" Star gasped. The wings on the tiny fairy were moving and made the air whisper the girls' names.

"No idea, but that's nothing compared to yesterday," Bird observed.

When the girls returned to their father, he and Brian were still talking about the developers and the Fells. "Money drives everything these days," their dad said. "And the judge seems oblivious to your claim? Seriously, Brian, is there really any way to stop the construction?"

"Money matters, but with the right people on our side we have a chance." At that moment, Bird looked up, and Brian smiled at the girls as if he knew their secret.

∾

"Ah, so you finally noticed the statute," Jasper grunted, as the girls followed him, weaving between the upper branches of the trees.

"What do you mean, finally?" Star asked, offended by Jasper's tone.

"I mean, finally. You block-headed humans never take the time to notice anything. We've had those statues planted in gardens all around the town ever since we made the deal with the dwarves." At this, the girls stopped weaving and shouted after Jasper.

"Dwarves? *Please.*"

He looped back, pleased with their ignorance. In a slow and falsely sweetened tone, as if he were speaking to a squirrel, and a not-very-intelligent squirrel at that, he explained. "We needed to find a replacement for Brian, so we contracted with the dwarves to make those statues. We placed them in the gardening centers all around the town and used our magic to monitor everyone who bought one. We figured anyone who bought one might also be interested in helping us."

"But, dwarves, do they really exist?"

Jasper looked at the girls as if they had suddenly turned into not-very-intelligent woodchucks, "Ughhh! Look at the landscape under you. What do you see? Granite boulders and boulders on top of boulders, and boulders in crevices, and stones, stones, stones! Boulders attract dwarves like clover attracts bees." He stared, baffled at the girls before saying, 'Hurry up. We've got work to do, and be quiet because we're about to spy."

The three wove through the trees, past Panther Cave, across the mud road and up toward a lookout tower. The tower was built of boulders. *Dwarf construction*, Bird thought as they approached. Inside, it had marvelous wooden beams and stone stairs, and from the top the girls could see all of Boston, the harbor, and far inland, past the edge of their town. But today they didn't climb the tower, they landed right on its steep roof.

Jasper motioned to them to keep quiet before pointing to a group of men below. "Watch," he whispered.

"Won't they see us?" Star asked.

"Of course not," Jasper harrumphed, "They call themselves businessmen."

"What does that have to do with anything?" Star questioned.

"Businessmen humans never see anything they don't want to see," Jasper looked at her as if she'd asked if the grass was green. "What do they teach you in school?" Star was about to defend her teachers, but Jasper just motioned for her to be quiet.

The three gazed down at the men. Two of them looked like average commuters taking a lunchtime stroll; they wore comfortable hiking shoes, khaki pants, and light blue button-down shirts, but the third seemed odd: he wore shiny black dress shoes, dirty khaki pants, a tuxedo jacket with a flannel shirt underneath and a bright red tie. Star, who was very fashion forward, giggled and pointed before Jasper pinched her arm and told her to listen to the conversation.

"See all those cars rushing by down there?" the man with the shiny black shoes pointed to the highway. "I see consumer-commuters, and each one of those stressed-out consumer-commuters wishes she had a place to go, a green place, a relaxing place. Look at this view. That commuter needs this view, but she needs more too. She needs a kale and strawberry smoothie, a salad of local greens, the sound of a Zen fountain and a sea-salt pedicure. And she needs it all to happen right here. Right here we can build it."

"Sounds nice," Bird whispered to Star, "like something Mom would like. We could get her a gift certificate for Mother's Day."

Jasper pinched Bird, "These are the bad guys," he spat.

"It's a great idea, and my investors are 100 percent behind you," replied one of the men in the khaki pants. "Green products and green living are very *now*, but how are we going to get approval from the park's commission and the court? This place has been protected for over one hundred years. I can't imagine they'll let us just bulldoze down the side of this hill to build an access road."

"And what about that citizens' group?" the other man in khakis asked. "My lawyer tells me they're trying to gather signatures to stop us."

"Don't worry about either," the man in the shiny black shoes said. "I have very powerful friends, and each agrees that profit means progress. Right now, what is this patch of rock and this useless tower providing? Nothing. A valuable location like this and all people do is hike up and leave? Please. Land should belong to the person who can make the most of it. Our plan will create jobs, offer a place for the stressed consumer to relax, provide luxury housing, and turn a useless patch of land into a valuable shopping center."

"I admit," said one of the khakis, "it's a great idea in an unstoppable location. If you get permission to build the access road to this tower, I'll get the money. But what about your brother?"

"Don't worry about him. We've already got the access road," the badly-dressed man replied. "We'll pave the trail and run an electric bus up. People love electric buses and kale pedicures."

"You mean smoothies," the first man said.

"Look at the view from here," the other man in clean khakis observed. "We'll have to knock down the tower, clear-cut the hill, and blast out some boulders to level this place, but, wow, can you imagine how much someone would pay for a condo with this view?"

"And, people love easy access to the highway," the oddly dressed man encouraged. "We'll build a parking garage, and the renters can bike up or take the electric bus. Green living in the Fells! What an idea." The three men turned from the view and began walking down into the Fells.

Bird turned to Jasper. "It's so terrible," she said, "They're making it seem good when it is really bad."

Star was watching the men walk away. "That one is weird," she said pointing at the man with the shiny shoes. "A total fashion disaster," she added, but there was something else.

"Star," Bird admonished, "They are talking about tearing down our park and replacing it with kale-sipping commuters and you are thinking about fashion! Really?"

Star pointed again. "No, I'm serious. Something weird is happening around his shoes." As the terribly dressed man walked down the path, the plants seemed to bend away from his shoes. "It's like he has fans in his shoes pushing the plants away," Star said.

"I've seen this before," Bird observed as the three flew away from the tower toward the fairy queen's castle. "Those plants aren't being blown by the wind; they are shrinking away from that man's feet." She paused. "And doesn't he look oddly familiar?"

CHAPTER NINE

Worse Than We Thought

"So," the queen looked sadly at Star and Bird, "it's worse than we thought. I thought they were just going to develop the old hospital site across from the park, but an access road right from the highway, a parking garage, the destruction of the tower, and a—what did you call it?"

"A green mall," Bird offered.

The queen frowned, "A green mall. I'm confused though. You say there were no smogrots swarming the men at the tower?"

"No," Star answered, "the air was clear." The queen looked at Jasper and the lines deepened around her mouth.

Jasper explained, "This is strange. Usually when humans destroy nature, they are swarmed by smogrots.

This is why the fairies have always remained neutral toward the human world. We figured their brains were damaged from the contact with the smogrots, and they weren't thinking."

"We couldn't conceive of any other explanation for why a creature would destroy the place where it lived," the queen added.

Jasper crossed his eyes and made a swirly motion at the side of his head.

"Thank you," the queen glared at Jasper. "But if these men weren't surrounded by smogrots, it means we are dealing with something more than mere stupidity." She paused. "We might be facing a true antagonist." She stared off into the distance for a few moments, lost in her own thoughts. "So, girls, what is your plan?"

Star and Bird explained how they had met Brian and volunteered to gather signatures for the citizens' lawsuit.

"If we gather enough signatures, the court will order the developers to stop," Star said.

"So, you decided to do this the human way?" The queen looked concerned.

"Is there another way?" Star asked.

"I wish I knew," she replied. "And I wish I knew why the humans are doing terrible things even when there are no smogrots surrounding them."

"I'm confused," Star said, "People do bad things all of the time. Why do there have to be smogrots around?"

"People often do terrible things, but rarely to themselves," the queen explained. "Think about it: the bully on the playground will tease and hit another boy, but it would be ridiculous if he hit himself."

"You're right," Bird observed. "Even on April Fool's Day, no one fools herself. You give the stick of pepper gum to someone else."

"We've been living in these Fells for centuries, and we're convinced that the way your world is now is a mistake," the queen continued. "People never hurt the land before they created the smogrots."

"How did the people create the smogrots?" Bird asked.

"It started when they filled in the bay and built buildings on top of it," Jasper grunted. "We saw these little stinky wisps slinking around wherever they would build a new building. Then they built the trains, then the cars, then the planes."

"All of this started as an accident," the queen added. "But once it started, each time the humans created a smogrot they were more likely to do something else that would create more smogrots. The humans are unknowingly working for the smogrots; they are destroying their home and turning their world into a place only fit for a smogrot."

"One thing is for sure," Jasper interrupted, "humans plus smogrots equals trouble for the Fells."

"And the world," the queen observed. "Now, when you go to gather the signatures, I want you to have this." She handed them a silky blue pouch tied with a golden cord. On the fabric there were gold embroidered wings.

"Wow, it's beautiful. Thanks," Star said, hoping for fairy jewels, or anything that sparkled. Truth be told, she had hoped for more bling in the fairy world.

Bird opened it and stuck her hand inside. "More fairy dirt, uh, I mean dust. This will be helpful?"

"It's a different kind," the queen answered, ignoring their disappointment, "Sprinkle some on yourselves before venturing out. It will let you see which humans are living with smogrots and which are still free. Let us know how each human reacts to your request when you return."

CHAPTER TEN

Signatures

"Seriously! Seriously!" Star complained, "Barbie gets wings, sparkles, and mermaid friends. Tinkerbell saves the world and helps the other fairies create spring, and what do we get!? A bag of dirt and a clipboard for gathering signatures! Fairies are way more fun in the movies." She shook her head before taking a handful of dirt and sprinkling it on her hair. "Ugh," she pouted and stared at herself in the mirror. "Real life stinks. This dulls my hair. Do you think the dirt will still work if I cover it with pink stripes?"

Bird looked at the wand of pink hair dye her sister held in her hand, "Worth a try. Where should we go first? I've never been good at talking to strangers. I couldn't even manage to sell 10 boxes of Girl Scout cookies."

Star was too busy with her hair. "How does it look?"

"Not bad, now how are we going to do this? I say we start with the nice people first."

"No way," Star smiled, she had a way with strangers and babies and dogs. "We treat it like a dinner plate. Always eat the icky food first so the best feels like a treat. Let's start with the most smog-rotted person we know and end with someone nice."

Bird was going to point out that Star had never, not once, ever eaten the "icky food" first, but decided it would be best to just move on with the plan. The girls tossed a bit more fairy dirt in their eyes and stepped outside. The neighborhood was transformed. A cloud of color surrounded each house. Some were yellow, others blue, some even rainbow, and a few were a grimy, greyish black. The girls looked at each other and understood what they saw: the colors showed the fairies how many smogrots lived in each house. Quickly, they turned back to see their own house. It radiated emerald green and a faint rainbow streamed out from the chimney. They smiled at each other and then headed for the place they wanted to go less than anywhere else on the planet.

The darkest house on the block belonged to Mr. and Mrs. Grades. When the couple first bought their little ranch house, Mrs. Grades was an art teacher and Mr. Grades was a landscape designer, but somehow things went awry: Mr. Grades and then Mrs. Grades went to law school. Now, they worked as corporate lawyers. A few years ago, they tore down their one-story ranch and built a three-story colonial-style mansion that dwarfed all the other houses in the neighborhood. They employed armies of gardeners, window washers, exterminators, and house cleaners to keep their house sparkling, but the girls knew, even before they got the fairy dirt, that the house would be crawling with smogrots.

The girls' parents had told them that when they were babies, before the ranch was knocked down, that they had been friends with the Grades. The girls refused to believe it until their mother showed them a photograph of the six of them sitting at an old red picnic table in Mr. and Mrs. Grades' now demolished backyard. Other than that time, their mother never talked about their neighbors, but once, when they were walking past and a lawn maintenance man was posting tiny yellow signs warning children and dogs to stay off the poisoned lawn, their mother shook her head sadly and said, "People who don't accept clover just can't be trusted."

Bird clutched the clipboard. "Why are we even bothering to ask for their signatures?" she asked Star.

Star shrugged her shoulders, "Did you quit the first time you tried to ride a bike?"

"No," Bird pouted. "But this is different."

"We've got to try," Star replied. "Think about how good it will feel if we succeed."

The girls walked up the cobblestone drive. Each cobblestone fit perfectly next to the other and petunias lined each side, but just as they suspected, clouds of smogrots circled the house like toxic tornados. "This isn't going to be easy," Bird said.

Star marched on, but her smile faded. "I feel a little sick just looking at them." They each took a deep breath of fresh air before wading through the smogrots up to the front door.

Mrs. Grades answered and told the girls it was "cute" that the girls were engaging in the democratic process, but she couldn't sign the petition because of a potential "conflict of interest." The girls were ready to walk away when Mr. Grades came bustling up behind his wife like an angry guard dog. "Bunch of crazy hippies trying to ruin the best business opportunity this town has gotten in 30 years!" He pointed to the girls. "The numbers are against you kids. We've got billboards and advertising and bulldozers." Mr. Grades's face was turning red and his eyes seemed narrow and yellow. Mrs. Grades put her hand on her husband's shoulder.

"Now dear, they have a right."

"They don't have a right to stop good business!" Mr. Grades spat as he spoke. His breath smelled like hot garbage. Star and Bird backed away as Mrs. Grades pushed her way outside and shut the door on her husband. For a moment, the girls saw something green and good flicker in her eye.

"Please forgive my husband," she said, "he just hasn't been himself lately." The girls managed to mumble good-bye and ran down the path. As they fled, the smogrots grew more powerful. Instead of swarming in circles around the girls, they nose-dived like furious wasps.

"It's trying to sting me!" Star shouted, "I feel sick!"

"Run!" Bird shouted back. The two ran down the path, their arms swatting the smogrots away from their arms and legs. Mrs. Grades stood at her porch watching and thinking that she'd have to call the exterminator again. They obviously had bees.

"Well," Bird observed, looking at her little sister, "That was nothing like riding my bike."

"Come on!" Star encouraged, wiping a bit of dark oily smudge from her arm. "Compared to that, the rest will be easy."

And it was. Most of the neighbors had heard of the plan for the green mall, but didn't understand that it was going to be built in the center of their nature preserve. A few didn't want to sign without talking to an adult first (the girls gave them Brian's name), but by lunch the girls had gathered almost another 100 signatures.

Bird was thinking about how exciting her "What I did over Summer Vacation" essay would be, when Star interrupted with, "That Mr. Grades sure is a terrible dresser."

"No, he isn't," Bird said, remembering the many times she had seen him decked out in suits and perfectly calculated weekend wear.

"Are you kidding? Didn't you notice?" Star always noticed fashion. "He was dressed like his closet exploded and he put on whatever hit him first." She giggled at her own joke.

"You can be the one to fix his fashion sense then, because I am never going back there. Not even for the Halloween candy."

"Just noticing," Star yawned. "These grown-ups are weird."

"Yeah, and I don't know how we are going to get enough signatures to stop the mall," Bird added. "We just asked everyone within walking distance of our house."

"It's time to get our bikes," Star suggested. Bird was about to explain that their parents would never let them ride all over town, when Star added, "and ride to the farmer's market." She pointed up into the sky. A halo of color, surrounded by a ring of green, was appearing over the downtown square. It was three o'clock on a Thursday. The farmers would be setting up their tents for the weekly market. "If we can't get signatures there, we can't get them anywhere."

CHAPTER ELEVEN

Another Visit with Brian

The next day the girls woke up brimming with optimism; they may have met a few strange grownups, but they had succeeded. Star had been right. The people who shopped at the farmer's market, and the farmers themselves, weren't tricked by the words Green Corporation. And, once the director of the market discovered what they were trying to do, he gave them poster boards and markers and let them set up a booth next to the face-painting and juggling. By the time the farmers packed up, the girls had the signatures they needed to bring a halt to the construction.

So, after a deep night's rest, the girls rushed down to breakfast, demanded waffles, and plotted the next step in their plan. The maple syrup hadn't even cooled in the pitcher when the girls arrived at Brian's house. Star was the first into the driveway, her bike tires skidding on the gravel as she swerved to a halt. "We did it!" she yelled.

Bird looked at her sister as if she had eaten crazy-pills instead of waffles. "Ahem," she counseled, "Star, there is no one here."

"An audience of one is enough for my victory," Star dropped her bike unceremoniously and walked up the stairs to the front porch. She pressed the bell twice to signal the urgency of the visit, and halfway through the second ring, Brian opened the door.

"We did it!" Star beamed, and Brian smiled back.

Although each had already eaten a waffle, the girls had room for cinnamon scones to accompany the story of their signature adventure. They told of the people who signed because they cared, the people who signed because they couldn't say no to kids, the people who signed with a look of surprise on their faces, the people who refused to sign, and the person who actually had the word "No" posted on the door for anyone who happened to knock.

"Those are the people who need to open their doors the most," Brian observed, before changing the subject and asking if they owned any clothing that wasn't either worn and sporty (Bird), or covered in glitter (Star).

"My mother tried to make me wear a button-down blouse for picture day," Star said, her mouth full of scone.

"And don't we have a few dresses in our dress-up bin that mom says we should wear to parties?"

Bird shrugged; if she couldn't paint in it or wear it to a softball game, it wasn't even worth considering. She scanned the room, trying to take her mind off of wearing a dress when her eyes landed on a photo of someone she knew. "That's the man we saw at the Fells Tower!" she exclaimed. Brian looked at the photo and all the energy seemed to drain from his body.

"My brother," he said, reaching for the photo with a shaking hand. "This is us in happier times." Star looked at the photo and tried to say something, but Bird interrupted.

"Why are you wearing matching clothes?" she asked.

"We were volunteering together at Fells Day," Brian brushed some dust from the glass. "See the matching vests?" Star giggled and Bird shot her a look that said she was absolutely not allowed to make fun of their matching vests.

Undeterred, Star continued, "This can't be the same person." She pointed at Brian, "Do you have more than one brother?"

"No," he replied, "Why?"

"Because this man has a sense of fashion and the man we saw in the Fells was one of the worst dressed humans I've ever seen."

"Impossible," Brian said. "Charles is always impeccably dressed. In fact, he won best dressed in our senior class."

The sisters looked at each other. Something very strange was going on.

"Well then," Brian said, obviously wanting to change the subject, "dig those dresses out of the bin. You are coming to court with me on Tuesday."

"What!" Bird exclaimed. "What could two kids possibly do for anyone in a court? A real court?"

"I'm not sure," Brian replied, "but there is something here that only you can solve. And, maybe you should leave those signatures with me. If the smogrots find out, you might not be safe."

Star straightened her back and shook her blonde hair, "What could the smogrots possibly do to me?"

CHAPTER TWELVE

Another Visit with the Fairy Queen

"Brian is obviously crazy," Bird shouted, as the two girls rode home.

Star stared steadily ahead, feeling differently than she ever had before. She stopped her bike and turned to stare at Bird. "He's not off his rocker," she said. "It's weird, but I've seen it before."

Bird stared at Star, giving her sister time to think. "What have you seen before?" she asked gently.

"The look in his eyes, when he said we were going to have to go to court. He looked like mom or dad when they had a present to give us. What do you think it is?"

Before Bird could answer, they both heard a loud pop, and Jasper appeared, flying round their bicycles in a state of total exasperation, "Watch out!" he screamed. They know you are working for us!" And, before the girls could protest their bikes took off into the sky. "Pedal!" Jasper shouted, "Fast!"

"What do you mean?" Star screamed. She looked down at her pedals. They were swirling faster than her feet ever could manage.

"Don't look back!" Jasper shouted. "Pedal!" The girls looked back and wished that they hadn't. A cloud of smogrots, green and grey, pursued them like a torpedo-shaped toxic swamp.

"Are those claws?" Bird shouted. The look on Star's face answered her question.

"They know," she mouthed, and her face turned grey, just like it had on the side of the road. Bird looked down and saw the cars on I-93 rushing past.

"Pedal!" Jasper shouted, "They gain strength over the highway!" Jasper turned around and the look of panic on his face when he saw Star made Bird feel sick. "Pedal!" he shouted again.

A wispy claw grabbed at Star's ankle and she turned the color of a dirty plastic bag; her eyes fogged over. "Jasper! Do something!" Bird shouted, reaching out to grab her sister. A smogrot's arm spun up Star's leg like a vicious snake. Just as Bird reached her arm around her sister, Star's hands let go of her handlebars, and her bicycle plummeted down into the Fells.

"Jasper!" Bird shouted. One hand grasped her handlebar and the other supported Star, who flopped over Bird's lap. The smogrot's claw slithered from Star's leg to Bird's waist. Suddenly, the sunny day was gone; Bird felt like she was trapped in a hot, wet, parking garage, and her hold on both Star and the bicycle loosened. "Jasper! Help! I can't. I'm dropping her." Jasper swooped down to the Fells and returned with something grasped tightly in his hand. He flew right over Star and dropped it on her head. Flower petals.

The smogrot let go as if it had been slapped. The sickness left Bird and her strength returned. She felt Star's hold on her tighten and she steered her bike down to the top of Panther Cave. The bike crashed to a stop in a group of low growing pine saplings, and the two girls flopped into the soft bed of pine needles, inches away from the top of the cave.

"Good thing that I'm the little sister," Star murmured.

"Huh?" Bird managed; she was exhausted.

"Good thing I'm the little sister," Star repeated.

"Why?"

"Just because," Star smiled, but Bird knew it was her way of saying thank you. Jasper hovered over the girls, impatiently, but let them rest for a few minutes until they were ready to walk into the cave.

"I'm not your queen," the Fairy Queen said, after they had found the secret passage (years of designing fairy houses had made Bird an expert). "I'm your partner." She explained that Brian was ready to retire and although he would continue to protect the Fells as a human, he knew he had to hand the job of protecting the magic of the Fells over to children. "Now," she said, "As your partner and queen, I must ask you a very serious question: what do you think of my dress?"

Both Star and Bird stared at the Fairy Queen's dress. It sparkled and shone in the light; it was purple and orange and green, and the colors blended together like a sunset on a hot August day. Best of all, the queen could *move* in the dress. As she spoke, she flitted around the throne room. Bird was sure she could have slid into third and stood-up without a wrinkle, and Star had never seen its equal on any runway. The Fairy Queen just nodded at them. Then a voice in their heads said, *Remember, in your world spirit exists on the inside, but in ours, it is only on the outside.*

The girls left the cave confused and bedazzled. They were tired, bruised, dirty, and not quite sure how they would get home.

"Mom's going to be worried," Star said.

"We really have given our parents a tough time," Bird added. The girls stood outside of Panther Cave, feeling overwhelmed.

"I feel the way I do when I think about the whole school year on the first day of school," Star said, looking to her older sister for advice.

"Me too," Bird replied, before the silence of the forest was interrupted by an angry little voice.

"Stop your whining and get up here," Jasper yelled. They ran up the path to the top of the cave. There, they saw a self-satisfied Jasper hovering next to two bicycles. Star ran to hug the little man, but he quickly dodged her embrace.

"You fixed my bike!" she exclaimed.

"Ha!" Jasper replied, "Not just fixed, better than new. While you were in there," he jerked his finger dismissively toward the cave, "talking about pretty dresses, I sent a team to retrieve and repair your bicycles."

"It's shinier than before! And, lighter," Star bounced the frame on her pointer finger. "Amazing."

"Yours is too," Jasper said, turning to Bird. "Now, get home. You have a big day tomorrow."

The girls leaped onto their bicycles.

"Air or ground?" Star asked.

"Let's see how fast these babies can travel the old-fashioned way!" Bird exclaimed.

"Agreed!" Star smiled back, "I need a break from flying." The girls sped down the path and toward their house. The bikes turned the corners so quickly they were nearly on their sides, but the new wheels never slid or skidded. The girls raced down the roads, marveling at fairy technology, turned into their driveway and unceremoniously dropped their bikes in the exact place their parents needed to park the car.

"That was awesome!" they exclaimed as they ran into the house.

After dinner, as they lay on their beds drawing, Bird was about to start a conversation about the court, when Star started talking about fashion.

"Did you see how the Fairy Queen *moved* in that dress? Why do you think that the prettier our clothes are the more they itch and pull and scratch? I wish we had clothes like the queen's. Why does everything about their world have to be prettier than ours?"

"Nothing will be pretty anywhere," Bird observed, "if we lose in court tomorrow."

CHAPTER THIRTEEN

The Court

The next day was Monday. Upon their request, their shocked mother dug their best dresses out of the toy bin and their surprised father washed the dresses in time for their appearance in court. The girls rode to the federal court with Brian and the lawyer for the Fells. "Don't worry girls," the lawyer assured them, "All you have to do is sit in the gallery with Brian. Just leave the rest to me."

But the girls weren't quite sure that was the case. Brian had given them a few looks that suggested the day would be more than uncomfortable dresses and watching.

The lawyer maneuvered the car into the carpool lane, but the girls weren't looking at the other cars, or the bridge that they loved that took them into Boston. Instead, they were wondering what would happen in the court.

They parked in a wide-open parking lot and walked toward the federal courthouse. Although it was a majestic brick building, full of windows and sitting right on the harbor, Star wished they were walking in the other direction toward the Boston Children's Museum, and Bird looked longingly at the Institute of Contemporary Art, remembering a much more fun day when she had chased her friend up and down the stairs at its front. As they walked toward the building, Brian picked up his pace and started looking straight ahead.

"Hey, Brian!" Star shouted, "wait up!" Brian rushed even faster. Star started to pout, but Bird tugged on her uncomfortable dress sleeve.

She pointed to the side at a group of men and smogrots walking across the parking lot, and there, right in the center, leading the way, was Brian's twin brother.

"Oh," Star said, her face falling. "Brian's brother is the head of the company."

"The Green Company," Bird added in a rare moment of dramatic emphasis.

"Don't worry." Star said. "We'll help him."

Wishes aside, the girls found themselves moving through security, then cramming into a crowded elevator, and finally filing into the trial court. If the girls had bothered to look around they would have found the room welcoming, with warm wooden walls and bright yellow lights, but, like almost everyone else who ever walked into the courtroom, they were too occupied with their own business to notice the lovely interior. They sat in the back until the judge said a few words they recognized, "Friends of the Fells versus Green Development Corporation," and a few they didn't.

"The fancy words are the ones that matter," Bird whispered to Star. Star just shrugged and pouted, thinking to herself that the court was dull, and her dress was scratchy.

"I wish our clothes were like the Fairy Queen's," she whispered back.

The lawyers started talking and Star started to drift off. Her boredom crept down to her legs and she had to kick her feet against the bench just to make sure that her legs would still move. She amused herself by tying and untying her shoelaces, and then counting the number of people with short hair (22) versus those with medium (six) and long (four) in the courtroom. This court was no place for a child. She assumed that her sister was equally bored, so it came as a shock when she noticed her sister looking intently at the judge. "What are you looking at?" she whispered into Bird's ear.

"Something is weird about that judge," Bird whispered back, just as Brian hushed them. The lawyers continued to speak, each taking a turn, and several witnesses were called, all speaking in grown-up language that hid what was actually happening. The judge kept saying the word "denied," but Star really didn't know what was happening or why it was so important that she was there. Star decided to watch her sister watch the judge. Then she decided to watch the judge, and she gasped so loudly that everyone in the court turned her way.

Shortly after her outburst, the judge banged his gavel and declared it was time for lunch.

As soon as they were out in the hall, Star grabbed onto Bird, "I know," Bird said in an excited voice. "He's a smogrot!" They walked up to Brian and the lawyer, both of whom had grim looks on their faces.

"It doesn't look good," the lawyer was saying. "And, it doesn't make sense. The judge just doesn't seem to want to allow any of our exhibits into evidence. Right now, I have to tell you, your case looks lost. I don't think we can stop those bulldozers." Brian shook his head. Star, who had yet to learn that most grown-ups don't listen to kids, interrupted.

"Of course, we aren't winning. The judge is a smogrot!" The lawyer looked at her as if she had said, "Yaks always stay away from peanut-butter laden mountain sides," or something else ridiculous like that. Brian, on the other hand, knew exactly what she meant.

"New kid slang," he explained, before adding, "You girls look hungry. How about lunch by the water?" The girls agreed, and the three walked outside of the court-house, leaving the lawyer to his documents and salad. Before they reached the exit, they passed Brian's brother. He stood in the middle of the defendants, smirking and gesturing. As they passed, he looked pointedly at Brian and said, "Tough day for the Fells. Good day for productive business."

Once they were seated at the restaurant, Star looked at Brian and dropped the big news, "The judge is a smogrot and so is your brother." She waited for his surprised reaction.

"Of course," he said, "the more important thing is, what we are going to do about it."

"You mean to tell me," Bird accused, looking at Brian as if he had hidden the last piece of a 1,000 piece puzzle, "that you knew all along that these people were contaminated with smogrots?" Luckily for Brian, the waitress delivered Bird's onion rings right as she was beginning her indignant speech, and, since her hunger outweighed her offense, she started to eat instead of lecture.

"Of course," he said again, reminding Star of Jasper, "I've noticed that a good many successful adults around here have the characteristics of a smogrot. If they all didn't have someone else dressing them they'd be easier to catch. These personal assistants are making things much harder for the fairies." He shrugged and ate a french fry, as if this wasn't news to the girls.

"But," screamed Star, who had little respect for decorum in public places, "what are we supposed to do!"

"Well," Brian mused, "You are both smart little girls."

"And slightly sassy," added Star.

"And, she has little respect for decorum in public places," added Bird. The three bent their heads together and made a plan.

CHAPTER FOURTEEN

The Dirt

"Is this really going to work?" Bird asked as the three walked back into the courtroom.

"It has to," Brian whispered back. "You know who is depending on it. Think of her." The girls looked at each other and knew there was no turning back. They had made a promise and, as their mother always said, *If you aren't going to do something then just don't do it, but the worst thing in the world is saying you will and then you don't.*

The court officer called the court to session. Star was so nervous she didn't notice the smogrot judge enter the room, or the developer's lawyer send an evil sneer in Brian's direction.

"Here goes nothing," whispered Bird.

Before she stood up, Bird remembered every fairy house she had ever built, she remembered gathering bark and painting leaves, and making rivers out of tin foil, and she remembered painting cardboard green and cutting apart greeting cards to make rugs. Then she remembered all the books she had read, and how she loved to make speeches at the dinner table. She remembered every time she had wanted to make a speech at school when she felt something was unfair but had held her tongue. And she stood up and called out to the judge. "My name is Bird and I'm here to tell you why what you're doing is wrong."

Then she told the truth. She told the judge about the pollution and the smogrots and how the smogrots were destroying the Fells and the fairies. She told him about how she had seen the flowers bend away from the foot of the smirking lawyer, and she told him that just because you call something "green" doesn't mean it is any good for the creatures that live in the woods.

On cue, just as Bird said, "Green doesn't mean good," Star ducked under the bar separating the trial from the gallery, snuck up to the bench, leapt into the witness chair and threw a handful of what appeared to be dirt into the judge's face. The judge stopped pounding his gavel and stared, momentarily stunned, before he flopped forward and his face hit the bench with a moist thump. Everyone in the courtroom froze. The judge's shoulders twitched

and an oily grey smoke seemed to rise from his head. Next, a terrible odor, a mixture of bleach, hot garbage, and car exhaust, filled the courtroom. The smoke swirled around the judge's head before darting across the court-room and out the door. The judge lifted his head like he was just waking from a deep sleep. With stunned eyes, he gazed up at Star, "Where am I?" he asked.

Star smiled up at him, trying to be as compellingly adorable as possible, and Bird answered, "You are in the courtroom about to decide whether these developers can build an access road through The Fells."

The judge glared at Bird as if she was the one who had just done something crazy, "Impossible," he said, "those developers had no claim to that land." Then he looked at the lawyers for the developers. "You had no claim. I told you that months ago. This case should be dismissed. In fact," and he lifted up his gavel in a very official man-ner, "this case is dismissed!" As Bird and Star cheered, the judge, recently returned to himself after months of being half-smogrot, told the court officer to cancel the day's cases and escort the developer's lawyers from the courthouse.

"Well girls," Brian beamed as they ran back to the right side of the courtroom, "you did it! How did you think to bring the fairy dust?"

"The heroes always need some kind of magical weapon to help them out of a tight spot," Bird replied.

"It was my idea!" Star protested.

"She's right," Bird admitted, "but the brilliant plan was mine!"

"Don't you have someone to tell someone about our success?" Brian asked, and the girls nodded, knowing they would soon be at Panther Cave.

CHAPTER FIFTEEN

The Beginning

The Fairy Queen smiled and thanked the girls. Then, as they all sat down to acorn-top tea, the girls asked, "Isn't there going to be some sort of award ceremony to reward us for our hard work and bravery?"

Jasper, who was serving the tea, snorted and mumbled something about "ungrateful, clumsy dirt-throwing humans," but the Fairy Queen smiled again and sipped quietly.

"Don't snort at me, Jasper," Star retorted, "I've seen many fairy movies and after the adventure there is always a grand awards ceremony." Jasper glared at Star again and jerked his thumb toward the door. "How rude!" Star began, but Bird interrupted.

"I get it," she said, "Star, don't yell at Jasper. He's trying to tell us that the Fells is our reward. Because we protected it, we still get to hike in it and ski and snowshoe and swim."

"And pick blueberries with Mom and Dad," Star finished.

"Exactly," the queen said, placing a tray of vanilla cakes decorated with candied mint before them, "but I must warn you, this is only the beginning. The smogrots are everywhere. I'm afraid that I might need you again."

"What do you mean?" Bird asked. "The judge said that the Green Corporation couldn't build the access road. It's over, right?"

"Unfortunately," the queen sighed, "In nature, nothing is ever over."

"Ugh," moaned Star. "Haven't we done enough? Aren't we supposed to get a medal and go home?"

"It isn't enough?" Bird asked, hoping for the answer she wanted to hear.

"Does the Green Corporation still exist?" the queen asked sadly.

"Yes," they answered.

"How many more plans do we need to come up with?" Star asked.

"That is up to you," the queen answered, looking like their mother when she told them she knew they would do the right thing.

The girls finished their tea, thanked the queen, and walked out from the castle. Each felt that odd last-day-of-school sadness.

"We are pretty good at coming up with plans," Bird observed after they'd crossed a stream. Star nodded. They both looked around at the Fells. The oak leaves were blowing in the summer wind, and the stream twisted between two lichen and moss-covered hills.

Without any fairy dirt, they both fully saw and understood the woods.

"Do you think there are any blueberries left in that pine stand?" Bird asked.

"Might as well go to see," Star replied. "After all, they are our reward."

The End

Wendy Pfaffenbach is a writer, teacher, and ex-lawyer who lives in Medford, MA with her husband and two children. Originally from upstate NY, she received her bachelor's degree from Union College and her J.D. from Boston University. Before becoming a teacher, she worked as a law-clerk in the Massachusetts Appeals and Superior Courts, and as a legal journalist for the trade journal, *Lawyers' Weekly*. She has taught English in the Concord Middle Schools, as well as History and Geography. She is a marathoner, mountaineer, boogie-boarder, and a lover of the outdoors. *The Fells Fairies* is her first book.

Julian Peters is a comic book artist and illustrator living in Montreal. In recent years, he has focused primarily on the adaptation of classic poems into comics. His most recent book is *Poems to See By.*
www.julianpeterscomics.com